Do you want a story,
Mr Barker?

FAIRYTALES
for MR BARKER

Jessica Ahlberg

WALKER BOOKS
AND SUBSIDIARIES
LONDON • BOSTON • SYDNEY • AUCKLAND

Lucy stopped reading.
Mr Barker wasn't listening to the story any more.
"Pay attention!" said Lucy, but Mr Barker was off.

"Where are we?" said Lucy.
A broken chair, three bowls of porridge
and a little golden-haired girl tucking in.

"Oh!" said Lucy. "I know where we are."

"This is the Three Bears' cottage,"
said Goldilocks. "Want some porridge?"
"No, thanks," said Lucy. "The bears might be home soon."

"Oh, dear. Do you think so?"
said Goldilocks. "They'll be cross with me."
"Then you'd better come with us," said Lucy, and off they ran.

"Where are we?" said Goldilocks.

Straw walls, straw ceiling, straw floor and three small pigs.

"Oh!" said Lucy. "I think I know where we are."

"This is our house," said the Three Little Pigs.

"Is it safe here?" said Goldilocks. "That sounds like a wolf."

"It is a wolf," said the pigs. "But we're building a new house out of sticks. That'll keep him out."

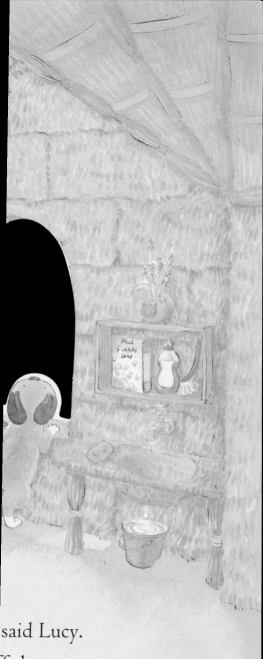

said Lucy.

f they ran.

"Wher
"Good
A gian
a gian
boy ca

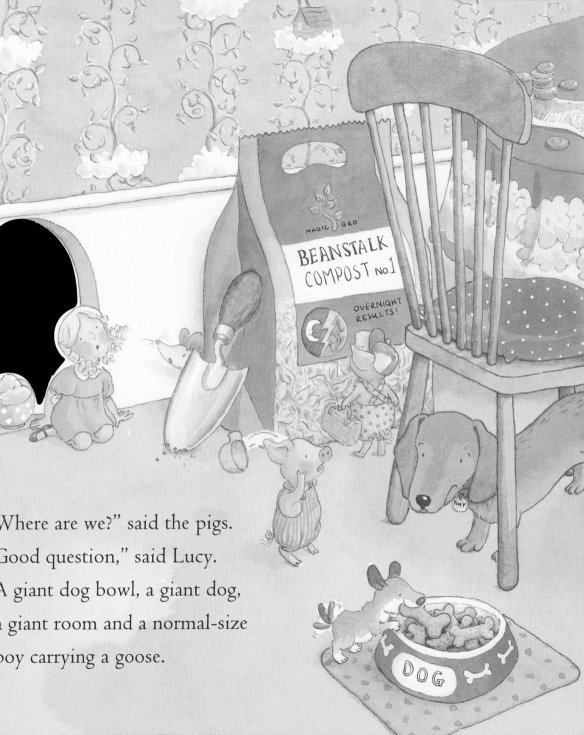

BEANSTALK
COMPOST No.1

MAGIC GRO

OVERNIGHT
RESULTS!

Where are we?" said the pigs.
Good question," said Lucy.
A giant dog bowl, a giant dog,
a giant room and a normal-size
boy carrying a goose.

DOG

CHINNY CHIN
CHIN RAZORS

MILD
SOAP

WOLF BE-
GONE!
WOLF PICKLES
TOXIC

BROWN
SUGAR

PLAIN
flour

"I don't think that's going to work," said

"You'd better come with us." And off they

"Oh!" said Lucy.

"I know where we are."

Fee, fi, fo, fum...

"This is the Giant's house, up the beanstalk,"
said Jack. "I'm borrowing his goose. It lays
golden eggs! But, *shh*! I haven't told him."

BORN TO BE BIG

"I think he knows," said Lucy.
"Uh-oh," said Jack.
"You'd better come with us,"
        said Lucy, and off they ran.

"Where are we?" said Jack.

A fancy bedroom (if it weren't for all the creepers),

a fancy bed and a little princess fast asleep in it.

"Naughty dog, Mr Barker," said Lucy.

"But I think I know where we are."

Sleeping Beauty yawned.

"This is my castle," she said. "What's all the noise?"

Then there was a CRASH!

"Oh, no," said Lucy. "Look who's following us!"

Three angry bears, a big bad wolf, a giant...
"And the bad fairy who put the spell on me,"
said Sleeping Beauty. "Help!"
"Quickly! You'd better come with us,"
said Lucy, and off they ran.

"Where are we?" said Sleeping Beauty.

A deep forest, a flash of red in the distance, a tower,
a funny little house made of sweets. And it was getting dark.

"I don't know where we are," said Lucy.
"But look who's behind us. I think we should hurry!"

Phew! Lucy closed the window behind them.

"Where are we?" said Goldilocks.

Books and toys, pictures on the walls and a dog bed.

"I know where we are," said Lucy. "This is my room!

You can stay for a sleepover and I'll read you a story."

"No fairies, no giants,
   no big bad wolves and no bears,"
   shouted everyone.
"Alright," said Lucy.
"Once upon a time
   there was a troll..."

For the baby

First published 2015 by Walker Books Ltd, 87 Vauxhall Walk, London SE11 5HJ
2 4 6 8 10 9 7 5 3 1
© 2015 Jessica Ahlberg
The right of Jessica Ahlberg to be identified as author/illustrator of this work has been asserted by her in
accordance with the Copyright, Designs and Patents Act 1988
This book has been typeset in Centaur MT
Printed in China
British Library Cataloguing in Publication Data: a catalogue record for this book is available from the
British Library
ISBN 978-1-4063-5588-8
www.walker.co.uk